DOODLE DANDIES

DOODLE DANDIES

doodle
poems that

w
o
r
d
s

J. Patrick Lewis

SCHOLASTIC INC.
New York Toronto London Auckland Sydney
Mexico City New Delhi Hong Kong

dandies
take shape

images

Lisa Desimini

with design and typography by
Ann Bobco
and
Lisa Desimini

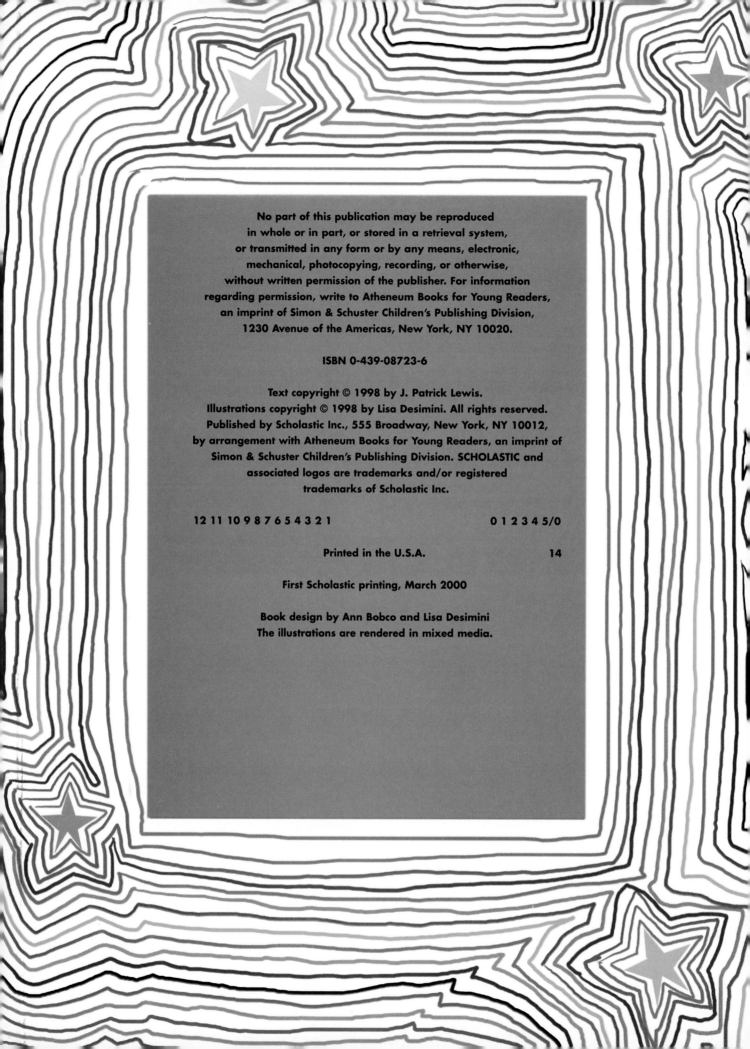

ISBN 0-439-08723-6

Text copyright © 1998 by J. Patrick Lewis.
Illustrations copyright © 1998 by Lisa Desimini. All rights reserved.
Published by Scholastic Inc., 555 Broadway, New York, NY 10012,
by arrangement with Atheneum Books for Young Readers, an imprint of
Simon & Schuster Children's Publishing Division. SCHOLASTIC and
associated logos are trademarks and/or registered
trademarks of Scholastic Inc.

12 11 10 9 8 7 6 5 4 3 2 1   0 1 2 3 4 5/0

Printed in the U.S.A.   14

First Scholastic printing, March 2000

Book design by Ann Bobco and Lisa Desimini
The illustrations are rendered in mixed media.

JUDE

—J. P. L.

FIONA

—L. D.

First Burst
of Spring

The day is cold, the earth is mud, but

don't let anything stop you, **B**ud!

Dachshund

Here comes the lady with the diamond ring
walking a dog like a sausage on a string
there goes the dog with his nose in the air!
walking the lady with the purple hair

giraffe

Tree-tall
giraffe

up to his neck

in brown and yellow
patchwork quilts, turns tail
and hobbles away
on wooden

stilts   stilts   stilts   stilts

The fastball
that you hope to poke
is smoke

The screwball
an ironic twist
hits your fist

A Swing and a Miss

The knuckler
wobbling up to you
can dipsy-do

The let-up pitch
you can't resist?
you missed

The curveball
that you thought was there
is air

The sinker
comes as some surprise:
it dies

The spitball
that by law's forbidden
(is hidden)

weeping willow

Her wind-woven hair softly sweeping

Her wind-woven hair softly sweeping

Her wind-woven hair softly sweeping

Her wind-woven hair softly sweeping

Her wind-woven hair softly sweeping

Her wind-woven hair softly sweeping

In
a far
field
of
sad
ness
stands
the
wee
wid
ow
wee
ping

Skinny **BONNIE** Bumber wears a long, tall hat. I hide her in the closet till the clouds get fat. I poke her up and out when the sun goes away. Fattie Bonnie Bumber

loves a rainy day!

umbrella

The butterfly is

the fantasy fulfiller of every caterpillar

day delights
in jungle cries

BIG
CAT

night ignites

its tiger eyes

synchronized
swim team

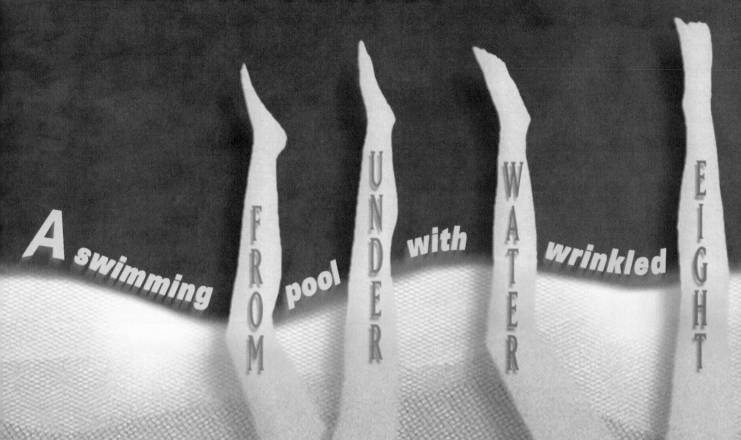

A *swimming* **FROM** *pool* **UNDER** *with* **WATER** *wrinkled* **EIGHT**

waves is PRECISION NEEDLES like a POKING quilt of THROUGH blue

The Oyster Family

An oyster boy, an oyster girl, an oyster dad, a mother-of-pearl

I slithered down to Pepper
Pond for
a midnight
snack, a
picker-
upper.
I missed
a mouse
and
beetle
bug,
so I
ate a
BULL
FROG
for my
supper.
Well, he
was tough
as toad,
and chewy.
Mighty
leggy,
mighty
lumpy.
And let
me tell
you,
Creep,
I'm
feeling
mighty
Jumpy!

Creep and Slither

winter

when sky unravels its cold mist-
eries

fluttering down brown skeletons of trees

these speckles on a page can barely show

the spectacle of unexpected snow

All eyes look down
the
cinder
track—
the
pole
vault
pole
connects,
bends
back . . .
the
boy
who's
hurled
above
the
bar
returns
to
earth
a falling
star.

Sky High

Mirror

You looking out
at me looking in—
I am an I-
dentical twin!
Did I just wink?
I thought I did,
because you flut-
tered your eyelid.
When one of you
makes two of me
there's twice as much
of us to see!

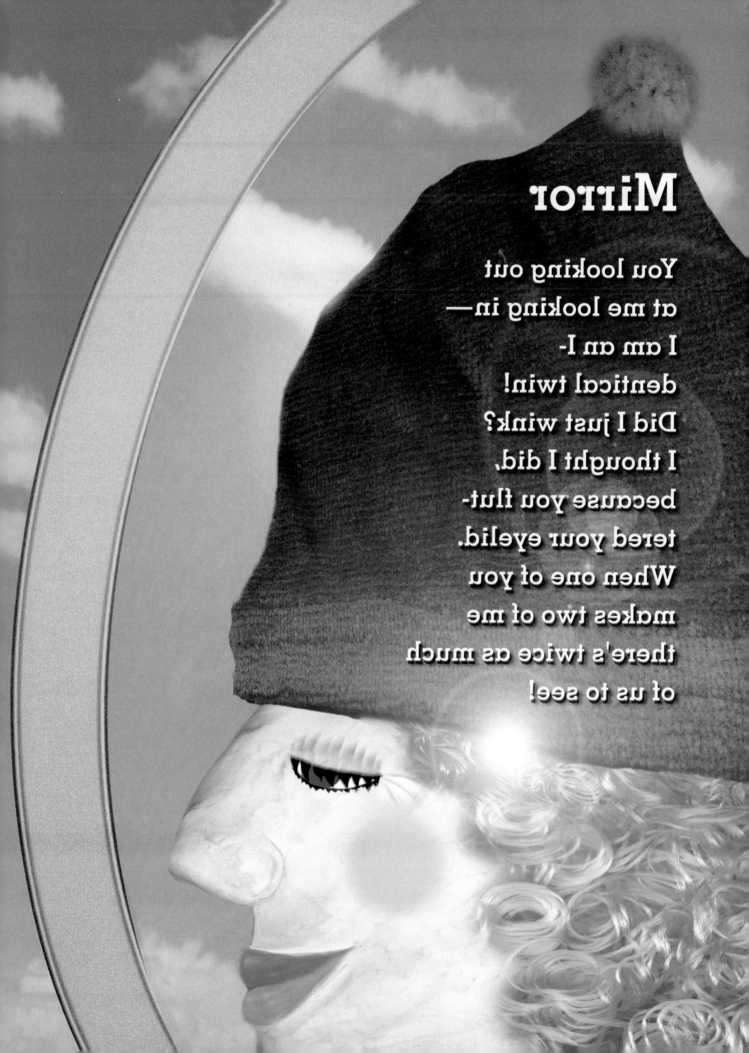

Mirror

You looking out
at me looking in—
I am an I-
dentical twin!
Did I just wink?
I thought I did,
because you flut-
tered your eyelid.
When one of you
makes two of me
there's twice as much
of us to see!

But the number of humps
on a camel grows,
and the bactrian is

extraordinary

 Off a

cming

Lashndra's

clck!

n the

sec nds left

Only

blck!

She takes a cr⬤ss-

c⬤urt pass

from y⬤u and

banks it off the glass f⬤r

tw⬤

LASHONDRA
SCORES!

SKYSCRAPER

I
am
a
nee
dle
of
steel
glass &
cement
1 0 2
s t o r i e s
high on a clear
day you can see
2 0 0
miles out into the
Atlantic or watch
hundreds of ants
scurrying like
people on the sidewalks
below & the yellow
bugs racing recklessly
along the city streets &
ride the elevator all the
way down in 37 seconds
FLAT

The Turtle

is a giant **hurdle**

I AM
A COSMIC
SNOWBALL MADE
OF DUSTY ICE AND GAS.
ONCE OR TWICE A CENTURY
I PASS THE EARTH AND
SUN. SEE YA NEXT
TIME AROUND . . .
IN 2061!

HALLEY'S COMET